BUS RIDERS

by Sharon Phillips Denslow
pictures by
Nancy Carpenter

 Four Winds Press
New York

Maxwell Macmillan Canada   Toronto
Maxwell Macmillan International
New York   Oxford   Singapore   Sydney

WATCH YOUR
STEP

Four Winds Press, Macmillan Publishing Company, 866 Third Avenue, New York, NY 10022
Maxwell Macmillan Canada, Inc., 1200 Eglinton Avenue East, Suite 200, Don Mills, Ontario M3C 3N1
Macmillan Publishing Company is part of the Maxwell Communication Group of Companies. First
American edition. Printed and bound in Hong Kong by South China Printing Company (1988)
Ltd.   10 9 8 7 6 5 4 3 2 1   The text of this book is set in Usherwood Medium.
The illustrations are rendered in oil paint and color pencil on paper. Book design by Christy Hale
Library of Congress Cataloging-in-Publication Data   Denslow, Sharon Phillips. Bus riders / by
Sharon Phillips Denslow ; pictures by Nancy Carpenter.   p. cm.   Summary: When their
regular bus driver gets sick, Warren, Louise, and the other bus riders must endure a string of
substitute drivers.   ISBN 0-02-728682-7   [1. School buses—Fiction.   2. Buses—Fiction.
3. Bus drivers—Fiction.]   I. Carpenter, Nancy, ill.   II. Title.   PZ7.D433Bu   1993 [E]—dc20   92-14109

2 Jun 93

To Kate, who told about the bus driver
with "toenails big enough for any kid to see"
and to Erin, who waited for her bus
through lots of cold, Lake Erie wind
and to all those kids who rode
the Benton school bus on the Mayfield
Highway long ago with me

—S.P.D.

For Virginia

—N.C.

Louise and Warren are the first ones on the school bus every morning.

They clomp up the steps, shouting, "Hi, Lee!" and sit in the crackly green seat directly behind him, taking turns on the inside and outside spaces.

Sometimes Lee says, "Morning," but usually he just closes the door, winks at them in the big mirror, and rolls the squash-colored bus on down the road.

Louise and Warren talk nonstop to the back of Lee's head.
"Did you hear about Wayne Pickles?"
"He cut his elbow!"
"And had three stitches!"
"And got a whole gallon of ice cream and a quart of strawberry pop because he got hurt."

Lee nods and sighs
and grunts
and "Uh-huhs" in response.

Wayne and the other wild Pickles boys, Donald, Dennis, Lloyd, and Mason, and their five dogs will get on the bus next.

As the bus tops Solomon's Hill and slowly begins its descent toward their house, Lee asks, "You all ready for the Pickles rush?"

"Bring on the Pickles!" Louise and Warren shout.

Then Lee opens the bus pocket and pulls out the Pickles Prize.

He waggles his eyebrows at Louise and Warren in the big mirror, and they waggle their eyebrows back.

The Pickles Prize is a candy bar. Today it's a Super Chocolate Supreme. Whoever guesses which Pickles dog will be the first one on the bus wins the Pickles Prize.

"Stow your lunch boxes," Lee says. "Secure your papers."

"Stowed and secured," Louise and Warren report.

"Then keep your legs out of the aisle and hang on!" Lee says.

As they pass the big white oak tree, the guessing game begins.

"Short Ribs!" Louise shouts, always picking the smallest dog.

"Fly!" Warren shouts back.

"Wipeout," Lee says with a nod. He tosses the candy bar into the bus pocket to await a winner.

The five Pickles boys hurl themselves toward the bus, followed by the five dogs, who have been lying around the porch, anticipating.

Wayne, Donald, Dennis, Lloyd, Mason, and Black Toe,
Short Ribs, Fly, Wipeout, and Quinn rush up the bus steps
and—sneakers thumping and toenails click-clacking—careen
to the rear.

"It's Fly by a nose!" Warren yells.

"Dogs!" Lee shouts in his hollow bass. The five dogs tear out of the bus and stand poised to chase it to the bridge while the bus riders cheer them on.

Warren thinks of his candy prize all day. It's the first one he's won in a week, and it's waiting for him on the bus.

But that afternoon when he and Louise climb up the steps, Lee is not in the driver's seat. A woman with brown curly hair and purple-and-green striped pants is behind the wheel. A big tag pinned to her blouse says "Thelma S."

"Let's get moving," Thelma S. says to Warren and Louise.

"Where's Lee?" Louise asks, not moving.

"Gallbladder. He'll be out three to four weeks."

Louise and Warren climb into their usual seat.

"What about your candy bar?" Louise whispers.

"She probably ate it," Warren says.

For a few minutes everything is quiet on the bus while everyone wonders about Lee. Then Donald hits Mason in the head with a notebook, and Mason thunks an eraser off Wayne's ear, and Dennis wrestles Lloyd to the floor, sending pencils and papers scattering under the seats.

"Active, aren't they?" says Thelma S.

"You missed your turn!" Warren shouts.

Thelma S. spends the week missing turns and bashing the Pickles dogs with her flowered purse.

WATCH YOUR
STEP

On Monday Willie is driving the bus.

"All right!" Mason says as soon as he sees Willie.

"He won't be a grandma driver," Wayne yells.

Louise whispers in Warren's ear, "Look at his toenails. They're big enough for any kid to see!"

"I wonder if he has a sweet tooth," Warren says, thinking about his Pickles Prize.

Willie has on a tank top, shorts, and sandals. He has a ponytail that bobs up and down and a boom box. Willie doesn't miss any stops or turns, and he yells at the Pickles dogs so fiercely that they run for the porch with their tails between their legs.

But the day after Wayne, Donald, Dennis, Lloyd, Mason, Louise, and Warren all wear tank tops and shorts and sandals to school,

Mr. Dodds, the assistant principal, is driving the bus.

Mr. Dodds wears a brown suit and a brown tie and wing tips. He has a short ruler that he raps on the dashboard when things get noisy. Mr. Dodds won't even open the bus door to let the Pickles in until Wayne and Mason take the five dogs to the backyard and tie them up.

"Do assistant principals like candy?" Warren asks Louise.

"Nah," Louise says, "and they don't like kids, either."

It is a long, quiet week on the bus.

Then on Monday, Louise squints as the bus pulls up.
"That's not Mr. Dodds driving," she says.
"I wonder who they've got now," Warren says.
    Then Louise looks at Warren and Warren looks at Louise,
and they begin jumping up and down. "Lee's back! Lee's back!"

"Hey," Warren says as the door opens, "we thought you'd never get back!"

"Me, either," Lee says, smiling, "but here I am. And I believe this is yours." Lee hands the Pickles Prize to Warren.

"I thought we'd go whole hog today," Lee says, holding up a bag of candy corn. "Winner take all."

"Short Ribs," Louise announces, not waiting for the big white oak.

"Quinn," Lee says, waggling his eyebrows in the mirror.

"Black Toe!" Warren shouts.

"Stow your lunch boxes," Lee says. "Secure your papers."

"Stowed and secured," Louise and Warren report.

"Well, then, keep your legs out of the aisle and hang on!"

The Pickles boys walk slowly toward the bus. Halfway there they stop and let out rebel yells, and in one thumping, bumbling, yelling eruption they rush to untie the dogs.

Free at last, Black Toe, Short Ribs, Fly, Wipeout, and Quinn race toward the bus, toward Louise and Warren and Lee.

"Go, Black Toe!" Warren yells.

"Come on, Short Ribs!" Louise yells back, already able to taste her chewy candy prize.